with the enormous turnip clutched in Grandfather's arms.

"Oh, my!" screamed the magpie.
"Look what I have done."
And he flew away to his tall tree.
From there he watched them
all lying flat on the grass,

"Now all together!" cried Grandfather.
And they all pulled with all their might,
and they pulled and they pulled and they pulled.
At once there was a loud noise
and the turnip came out of the ground
so suddenly
that they all fell down.

Just as Grandfather was about to give the signal
for them all to pull at the turnip,
a magpie who lived in a tall tree flew down
to help and pulled at the pig's tail.

"And that means you too, Samson!" they all yelled to the lazy pig.
The pig took such a big breath that he almost blew
the curl out of his tail and got ready to pull with the others.

Grandfather wiped some more sweat from his
brow and wrung out his beard.
"We will try once more—and all of you pull."

And they all pulled and they pulled
and they pulled.
Soon they were all out of breath.
But the turnip did not move.

Grandfather wiped the sweat from his brow.

"No old turnip is going to beat me," he growled..

"We will try again. Now all together."

So everyone got ready to pull.

The pig took a deep deep breath, the rooster ruffled his

feathers and the gander honked, as Grandfather counted:

"One...two...three...PULL!"

Now there was only the pig who was not pulling.

He was a very big, fat pig.

Grandfather shouted, "Get that lazy old pig! Make him pull with us!"

So Samson, the pig, came and pulled at the hen, who pulled at

the rooster, who pulled at the geese, who pulled at the cat, who

pulled at the dog, who pulled at Micky, who pulled at Grandmother,

who pulled at Grandfather, who pulled at the turnip.

"All together now," shouted Grandfather. "One…two…three…PULL!"

So they pulled and they panted and they pulled

and they pulled and pulled.

But the turnip did not move.

And they pulled and they puffed and
they pulled and they pulled.
But the turnip did not move.

The rooster and the hen came
and pulled behind the geese.
"Now all together!" shouted Grandfather.
"One...two...three...PULL!"
So the rooster and the hen pulled at the geese,
who pulled at the cat, who pulled at the dog, who
pulled at Micky, who pulled at Grandmother,
who pulled at Grandfather, who pulled at the turnip.

Seeing them all pulling and sweating and panting,

Ulysses, the cat, came and pulled behind Ringo.

And they all pulled and pulled and puffed and pulled.

But the turnip did not move.

Then Patrick, the gander, and the other geese came to help

and they formed a goose chain and they pulled with the others.

And they all pulled and they pulled and they pulled.

But the turnip would not move.

"This stubborn turnip, it's laughing at us!" shouted

Grandfather, wiping the sweat from his brow.

"Get the rooster and the hen. They can pull."

Ringo, the dog, came and pulled at Micky and they all pulled
and pulled and pulled until they couldn't pull any more.
But the turnip did not move.

Grandfather wiped the sweat from his brow.

"Call Micky to help us," he said.

Micky, their grandson, came and they all pulled

and they puffed and they pulled

until they could not pull any more.

But the turnip did not move.

"Get the dog to help," said Grandfather

when he had his breath back.

Grandmother came running, pleased that
Grandfather had asked her to help him pull.
"We will pull OUR turnip!" she cried.
So they pulled together and pulled and pulled
until they were both out of breath.
But the turnip did not move.

Then Grandfather called Grandmother
to help him pull the turnip.

The next morning Grandfather made up his mind
to pull the turnip to surprise Grandmother.
"It is so big," he thought, "that the neighbors'
silly goat will start eating it."
So Grandfather pulled and pulled until
he could not pull any more.
But the turnip did not move.

The turnip grew enormous.

One morning Grandmother awoke very early.

"I will pull that turnip before those greedy birds

eat it," she said as she hurried to the garden.

So she pulled and she pulled until she

was so out of breath she couldn't pull any more.

But the turnip did not move.

"Ho! Ho!" laughed Grandmother. "Your turnip indeed. It's my turnip. Didn't I water it every day?"

"Ho! Ho!" shouted Grandfather. "I planted it, didn't I? So it's my turnip."

The turnip got bigger and bigger.
"My turnip is beautiful!" cried Grandfather.

Grandmother watered it every day.

Grandfather planted a turnip in his garden.

FOR JERZY

THE TURNIP

STORY AND PICTURES BY
JANINA DOMANSKA

THE MACMILLAN COMPANY
COLLIER-MACMILLAN LIMITED, LONDON

PLEASE WASH
YOUR HANDS
BEFORE YOU READ ME
AND KEEP ME CLEAN

E

DATE DUE

2nd card

E

Domanska, Janina
The Turnip

	252
JUN 2 1990	
JUL 1 4 1990	213
AUG 2 5 1990	265
MAR 2 3 1991	432
	161